Elliot's
BATH

To my sister Debbie, who first inspired me to make toys

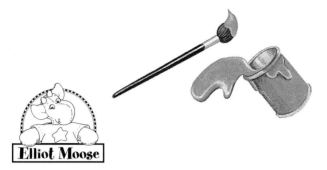

Elliot Moose

Elliott Moose™ Andrea Beck Inc.
Text and illustrations © 2000 Andrea Beck Inc.

Kids Can Press acknowledges the financial support of the Ontario Arts Council, the Canada Council for the Arts and the Government of Canada, through the BPIDP, for our publishing activity.

Published in Canada by
Kids Can Press Ltd.
29 Birch Avenue
Toronto, ON M4V 1E2

Published in the U.S. by
Kids Can Press Ltd.
2250 Military Road
Tonawanda, NY 14150

The artwork in this book was rendered in pencil crayon.
The text is set in Minion.

Edited by Debbie Rogosin
Designed by Karen Powers
Printed in Hong Kong by Book Art Inc., Toronto

The hardcover edition of this book is smyth sewn casebound.
The paperback edition of this book is limp sewn with drawn-on cover.

CM 00 0 9 8 7 6 5 4 3 2 1
CM PA 01 0 9 8 7 6 5 4 3 2 1

Canadian Cataloguing in Publication Data

Beck, Andrea, 1956 –
   Elliot's bath

"An Elliot Moose story"
ISBN 1-55074-802-5 (bound)   ISBN 1-55337-070-8 (pbk.)

I. Title.
PS8553.E2948E433 2001   jC813'.54   C00-930765-6
PZ7.B32E1 2001

NELVANA

Kids Can Press is a Nelvana company

Elliot's BATH

Written and Illustrated by
ANDREA BECK

KIDS CAN PRESS

Elliot Moose felt all tingly inside.

The big talent show was tonight!

He and Socks had been rehearsing all week. Their dance was perfect and their costumes were ready.

Now all they had to do was paint the stage.

"I'm almost done!" called Socks from her ladder.

But as she reached over with her brush, she lost her balance and tumbled to the floor.

SPLAT!

Elliot gasped.

He and Socks were covered in blue paint!

"What are we going to do?" cried Socks.

"You need a bath!" said Paisley.

A bath? Elliot had been damp before. He'd even had his paws in the pond. But he'd never had a bath.

"That sounds like fun!" he said with a grin.

Beaverton came over to survey the damage.

"Goodness gracious!" he exclaimed. "What a pickle! Let's wash you before that paint dries."

They all ran to the bathroom and, one by one, they climbed up to the sink. Angel put in the plug. Paisley turned on the water. And Beaverton tossed in the soap.

The bath was ready.

Elliot dipped his foot in the water.
It was perfect — not too hot and not too cold.
He and Socks jumped in.

Socks paddled around the sink. Elliot splashed
and spluttered. Together they made great, big waves.

Then they settled down to wash.

The warm water soaked right through Elliot's fur
and into his stuffing. It felt rather nice!

Soon the water was blue with paint and Socks
began to change color. As they soaked and scrubbed
she got darker and darker. Socks didn't mind at all.

"Purple!" she cried. "My favorite!"

But then something odd happened — Elliot's arms and legs began to get heavy. Soon, even his head felt funny.

"I think we should get out now," he said.

But they couldn't get out.

They couldn't even pull the plug.

Elliot and Socks were too full of water to move.

"Hmmm," said Beaverton.

He went to get his fishing rod and rain gear. Then he snagged the plug and tugged until it came free.

He tossed a raincoat to Paisley, then hopped into the sink.

"I'll push and you pull," he said.

Grunting and groaning, Beaverton and Paisley heaved their soggy friends out of the sink.

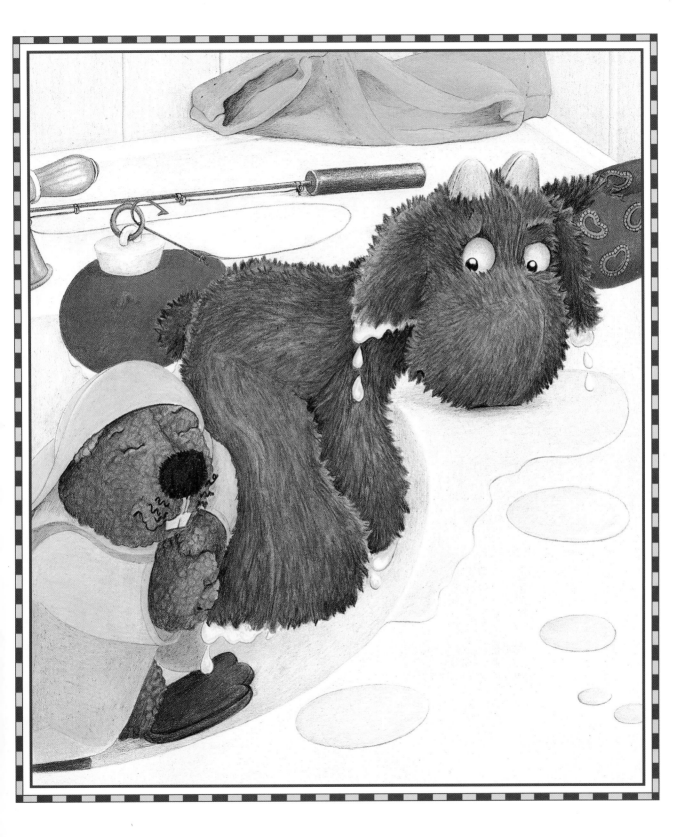

"Let's get you dry!" said Paisley.

He rolled Elliot and Socks up in towels and gave them each a good squeeze. But when he unrolled his friends, they were still soaking wet.

Elliot looked at the puddle forming beneath him and had a terrible thought.

Would they be dry in time for the show tonight?

"A breeze will evaporate that water," said Angel, flapping her wings. But her wings only made tiny puffs of air. It wasn't nearly enough.

Paisley got his airplane and wound up the propeller, but the wind made Socks shiver.

"It's too cold," she cried.

Next, Beaverton blasted them with the hair dryer. It made Elliot's ears sting.

"It's too hot!" he yelped.

By now, news of the bath had spread through
the house. A crowd of friends began to gather.
They talked in worried whispers.

"I'm sorry I splattered you," said Socks quietly.

"It wasn't your fault," said Elliot.

But he was sorry, too.

"There *must* be a way to get them dry!" said Paisley.

"We can't dry their outsides because their insides are too wet," reasoned Beaverton.

"We could *wring* them out," said Angel. "Like this!" She twisted a wet towel until water dripped out.

"You can't wring us out like laundry!" said Socks indignantly.

Laundry?!

Elliot's ears pricked up. Suddenly he knew just what to do!

"Get the wagon!" he shouted happily.

"Ready. Set. GO!" yelled Beaverton. And he sent Elliot and Socks swinging out on the clothesline into the hot sun.

"Elliot!" cried Socks. "We're flying!"

"And we're drying!" yelled Elliot.

Swinging on the line was so much fun that Paisley and Angel had a ride, too.

By the end of the afternoon, Elliot and Socks were dry. And to everyone's delight, Socks had kept her new color.

When Beaverton reeled them back in, they all rushed off to get ready for the show.

Elliot and Socks put on their costumes and practiced one more time.

That night, the two dancers twirled joyfully across the stage.

As Elliot and Socks took their bows, their friends clapped and cheered, and shouts of "Bravo!" rang through the halls of the big house.